The Deadly Power of Medusa

The Deadly Power of Medusa

Will Osborne and Mary Pope Osborne

Inside illustrations by
Steve Sullivan

AN
APPLE
PAPERBACK

SCHOLASTIC INC.
New York Toronto London Auckland Sydney

For Malcolm Groome

ISBN 0-590-45580-X

12 11 10 9 8 7 6   2 3 4 5 6 7/9

Printed in the U.S.A.   28

1

ꙮꙮꙮꙮꙮꙮꙮꙮꙮꙮ

The King's Great Fear

A thick mist hung over the stone shrine of the Oracle of Delphi. In the distance, snowy mountain peaks glowed with the pink light of dawn as King Acrisius knelt before the altar and bowed his head.

"What is your question?" The Oracle's voice seemed to come from deep in the earth.

The King of Greece raised his head. "I am growing old," he said. "I do not fear death, for my life has been rich and my kingdom is great. But I fear all will have been for nothing if I have no son to inherit my throne."

"Foolish ruler," boomed the Oracle,

"why do you dwell on what you do not possess instead of rejoicing in what you have? You have no son, but your daughter is strong, loyal, and beautiful. Why will you not be content that the gods have blessed you with such a beautiful, loving child?"

"Because I want a son!" cried Acrisius. "A *boy* to inherit my kingdom! A boy to raise in my own image! Do not call me ungrateful; just tell me: Will I have a son?"

A damp wind stirred the mist. The Oracle glared deep into Acrisius' eyes. "You will have no son," she said, in a voice as cold as the morning air. "But fear not, arrogant mortal, there will be an heir to your kingdom. Your daughter Danae *will* bear a son; hers is the child who will inherit your throne."

"Aaah," breathed the king. "A grandson."

"Wait!" called the Oracle. Her voice echoed through the mountains. "You

6

rejoice too soon. There is more to my prophecy. Yes, you will have a grandson. He will grow to be a man. And you will die by his hand."

"What?" roared the king. "I am to be murdered by my own flesh and blood? Surely it is not possible!"

The mist began to swirl about the Oracle. "I have done your bidding," she said. "I have looked into the future. The prophecy cannot be changed. . . ."

"But. . . ."

The Oracle had vanished, leaving her deep voice echoing through the hills: "The prophecy cannot be changed . . . cannot be changed . . . cannot be changed."

The king's minister shook his head. "No, Sire," he said, "the Oracle has never proved false."

Acrisius paced back and forth in his royal chamber. "Never?" he said. "Then must I submit like a sheep to this . . .

this curse? No! I shall not! There must be a way. I will offer sacrifices to the gods every day. I will journey to the foot of Mount Olympus. I will walk barefoot there alone, and throw myself on the gods' mercy! I will — "

"Sire," said the minister, "the prophecy cannot be changed."

Acrisius wheeled on the minister, his fists raised. "Do not say so!" he roared. "Do not repeat those words to me ever again! I *will* change the prophecy!"

Acrisius took up his sword and pushed past the minister into the corridor. "My grandson will not murder me, for I will have no grandson! I will kill his mother before he is born!"

Acrisius stormed down the corridor to Danae's chamber and pounded on her door.

"No, Sire, you must not!" cried the minister, running after the king. "The gods would never forgive you for slaying your own daughter! It is unthinkable!" He wrestled the sword from Acrisius' hand. "Put your sword away, Sire! It is unthinkable."

At that moment Danae's handmaiden opened the door to the young girl's chamber. She bowed deeply to the king, and Danae looked up from her spinning. When she saw her father, a smile of joy crossed the young girl's face.

"Father! You have come to visit me!" Danae rushed to embrace the king, and the old man's heart melted at her touch. "Why have you come so early in the day?"

Acrisius looked guiltily at the minister as he stiffly returned Danae's embrace. "I . . . I only wished to see what you were weaving," he stammered, pulling free from her arms. "Go back to your work . . . I'm sorry to disturb you . . . I'm sorry. . . ."

Back in his chamber Acrisius wept bitterly. "What am I to do?" he moaned.

"Must I live at the mercy of an unborn child? Is there nothing in all my vast kingdom to save me from my fate?"

The king rose and walked to the window. He gazed across the palace grounds: his courtyards, his sculptures, his towers. Finally his gaze rested on a corner of the garden where the royal carpenters were building an aviary to house his collection of exotic birds.

"Wait," said the king, turning to his minister. "I cannot kill my daughter. But if I can keep her from the world . . . if I can confine her so she can never marry nor bear a child. . . ."

"Cage her like an animal?" said the minister. "She would be better dead!"

"Not like an animal!" roared the king. "Caged, yes, but like a royal princess! In a bronze chamber beneath the earth. She will have the finest of everything, the most splendid quarters my workmen can create! But she will see no one! And she will never bear the son who was to be my murderer!"

"But Sire — "

"Silence! I have found my answer! Call my carpenters, my stonemasons, and my metalworkers to me! Go!"

The king clapped his hands. "Ah, Zeus, your laws are strict, but I have beaten you! I must not kill my daughter, no, but she will have no son! I will see to it! She will have no son!"

And so the great bronze chamber was built. Sunk forty feet into the earth, it was lit by a single skylight high above Danae's bed. Around the skylight were holes to let in fresh air, and a small door in the ceiling was provided for lowering food and water inside. Once the roof was sealed, there was no passage into the chamber large enough to admit another human being; even so, the grounds around the skylight were guarded by fierce dogs and no one but the king and his minister was allowed even to gaze through the window. And it was in this lonely, enforced solitude that Danae spent her days and nights weaving, sleeping, and weeping over her cruel fate.

"Oh, gods, I am already buried, now let me die!" cried Danae. "I would rather be dead than live out my life in this loneliness!"

The tiny window high above her bed revealed an early evening sky. Soon it would be dark, and Danae dreaded spending another night alone in her prison. She could hear the sounds of birds chirping far away, and the voices of peasant women in the courtyard hurrying home to their hearths. These sounds that had once brought her joy now only made her ache with loneliness. Danae threw herself down on her bed.

"I wish my father *had* killed me!" she wailed. "I do not wish to live like this. I do not wish to live at all!" Danae buried her head in her pillow and wept. As the light in her shadowy cell faded to darkness, she fell into a troubled, exhausted sleep.

At midnight, a clap of thunder awakened Danae. She sat up in her bed and looked around her. This must be a dream, she thought, for the chamber was filled with a shimmering golden light. But then the room began to shake and the light grew brighter and brighter, until Danae was suddenly aware that she was in the presence of Zeus, king of the gods. She closed her eyes as the light of Zeus passed through her body.

And in the morning, when the birds began to sing and rosy dawn crept into the bronze chamber, Danae gave birth to a baby boy.

"A grandson?" the king shrieked. He grabbed the minister and shook him roughly. "What do you mean, man? That is impossible!"

"It is true, Sire. A beautiful baby boy. She calls him Perseus, and claims he is the son of Zeus. I have seen him with my own eyes!"

Acrisius pushed the minister away and sank to his knees on the marble floor. "Oh, Olympus, why do you torture me?" he wailed. "I have spared her life, I have built a magnificent chamber for her, I have done nothing to offend the gods — and now you mock me? Zeus, I curse you!"

"No, Sire," cried the minister, "you must not say such a thing. The gods — "

"Silence!" Acrisius bellowed. "I defy the gods! Call my carpenters again! Have them build a chest large enough for a mother and a newborn babe. Then seal my daughter and her . . . her . . . Olympian offspring in the chest and hurl it into the sea!"

"But, Sire, they cannot survive! They will surely die!"

"Ah, but not by *my* hand! If she and

the boy should perish at sea, it will be the will of the gods. Let the gods be responsible! Now go!"

"But, Sire — "

"Go!"

2

The Old Fisherman

Danae hugged her baby closer to her breast as another wave rocked the wooden chest. She did not know how long they had been floating on the sea. The darkness made it impossible to tell day from night, and she had long lost her sense of time.

The baby Perseus stirred in her arms, but made no sound. He is too weak now even to cry, Danae thought. Soon he will die in my arms. She began to weep as she felt her baby's tiny hands clutching her in the darkness. "My own little child," she whispered through her tears. "You will never see the light of a spring

17

morning, never know the joy of running along the beach in the fresh open air, chasing the gulls ... never know, never know...."

Danae hugged Perseus tightly and closed her eyes. "But at least we shall die together," she whispered. "And be together with the gods...."

Too weak to go on, Danae passed into a deep, deep sleep.

Gulls cried out in the fresh morning air as the old fisherman Dictys picked his way along the shore. "Yes, a good day, a very good day," he said, squinting over the waves toward the sunrise. "A bad day for the fish, perhaps, but good for the man who goes to catch them, eh?"

Dictys turned from the sunrise and headed up the beach. "Ah, what's this, what's this?" he said when he saw the chest. It was covered with seaweed and half buried in the sand. "Look what the

sea has brought us today! What do you suppose is inside? Gold? Treasures? Perhaps some exotic spices from another land? Let us find out. . . ."

Dictys found a large rock and began hammering at the chest's heavy lock. After a few blows the lock gave way, and Dictys lifted the lid to reveal Danae and Perseus inside.

"Oh, my word," he cried when he saw the mother with the baby nestled in her arms. "Was this a coffin cast out to sea? Or do they live?"

Dictys gently lifted Perseus from his mother's arms. Roused from his sleep, the child began to cry, and hearing her baby as if he were crying far, far away, Danae struggled to open her eyes.

"Are you a god?" Danae said when she saw Dictys holding Perseus and peering down at her. "Are we in heaven now?"

Dictys laughed. "No, my dear, unless heaven is a land full of poor old fishermen. But you are safe now, and alive — and so is your beautiful child."

Danae looked into the kind old fisherman's face and her eyes filled with tears.

"Then you are wrong," she said. "I am in heaven after all."

Dictys took Danae and Perseus to his cottage and, with the help of his wife, nursed them back to health. Having no children of their own, the old fisherman and his wife welcomed the mother and her child into their home, where the four lived happily together as a family.

The years by the sea passed swiftly, and Perseus grew to be a strong, happy young man. Dictys taught him to fish; and every morning at dawn the two would haul Dictys' nets down to the shore where Perseus would spend the day at the old man's side, listening to his tales of the ocean.

Danae never revealed that she was

the daughter of a king, nor that her boy was the son of Zeus. Her days were spent helping Dictys' wife cook, garden, mend the nets, and tend the house. And at night, in the sleepy evening hours, she would take long walks on the beach with Perseus. Watching the moonlight dance on the waves, she felt a freedom and happiness she had never known before.

Danae hummed softly to herself as she lay the damp clothes on the rocks to dry. The morning was hot, but the salt breeze from the sea felt cool and fresh on her bare arms. When she had spread the last piece of clothing out on the rocks, she rose and stretched her long, graceful body in the sun. The wind tossed her silky golden hair, and she paused for a moment, silhouetted against the sea, and breathed the fresh salt air.

It was at that moment that Polydectes, the greedy, selfish ruler of the island, first saw Danae — and decided he must have her for his wife.

Polydectes' horse snorted and pawed the ground, but the king jerked roughly on the reins. He could not take his eyes off the beautiful young woman as she turned from the sea and ran lightly toward the old fisherman's cottage. How extraordinary, he thought. A mere peasant woman, but fit to be the bride of a king. . . .

Polydectes' thoughts were interrupted by the sound of footsteps on the road behind him. The king turned to see young Perseus carrying an armload of nets. Perseus nodded politely and turned off the road onto the path that led to the cottage.

"Hold, boy!" Polydectes called. Perseus stopped and looked back. He did not like being called "boy," but Polydectes was ruler of the island, and Perseus knew he must obey his king.

"Boy, do you know the young woman who lives in that cottage?"

Perseus bristled. There was something in the king's voice that made him uneasy. "Of course I know her," he said. "She is my mother."

"Ah, I see," said Polydectes. A crooked smile crossed his face. "And where is your father?"

Perseus glared at Polydectes. "I have none," he said. "Why do you want to know?"

Polydectes didn't answer Perseus' arrogant question. The smile vanished from his face, and the two glared at one another for a long moment. Then Polydectes spurred his stallion and galloped past Perseus back toward the city.

3

The Terrible Promise

In the days that followed, Perseus could not get his encounter with Polydectes off his mind. He did not like the way the ruler had asked about his mother, nor the twisted smile that had crossed the king's face when Perseus had told him there was no father in the house. But as the summer wore on and the days passed as usual, the incident began to seem less important until Perseus had almost forgotten it entirely. And then the message arrived.

"Well, my boy, it is an honor, an honor indeed," said Dictys when Perseus told him of the invitation. "It is not every day that one gets invited to a king's banquet. No message came to invite *me* today, I can assure you! Yes, it is a great honor."

"I suppose so," said Perseus. "But I wonder why he chose to invite me."

"Perhaps he only wishes to know his subjects better," said Dictys.

"Or perhaps he has a niece who needs a strong young husband," said Dictys' wife.

Danae laughed. "Oh, yes, that must be it!" she said. "We forget how handsome you've become. I'm afraid I still think of you as my baby boy."

Perseus shrugged and turned away. Perhaps they were right. Still, he remembered the king's cold stare when they had parted on the road, and the invitation made him uneasy. No, he didn't trust Polydectes. He would go to the banquet, but he would keep a wary eye on the king.

*   *   *

To his surprise, Perseus was having a good time at the party. The king had greeted him warmly, with none of the hostility Perseus had felt in their encounter on the road. Perseus had been introduced politely to the other guests, and at dinner he found himself enjoying the food and the lively conversation at the table. After the final course was served, one of the courtiers rose and called for attention.

"I trust we have all enjoyed this feast at our king's table," he said, and the guests all voiced their agreement.

"Well, we have received our bounty from the king; now it is time to celebrate the king with our gifts! First, let us drink a toast to Polydectes, and then our gifts will show him how we honor him!"

The guests all raised their glasses and Perseus looked around, confused. His invitation had said nothing about gifts!

After the toast, the courtier turned to the guest on his right. "Now, let the presentations begin with you, Carpetus," he said. "What have you brought for our king?"

"My king, I am happy to present you with six of the finest stallions in my stables," said Carpetus, bowing to Polydectes. "May you enjoy them in good health and great happiness." All the guests applauded, and the king nodded in appreciation.

One after another, the guests rose to make their presentations to the king; and each gift seemed more magnificent than the last: golden treasures, sculptures, a sailing vessel. With each presentation Perseus felt his embarrassment grow. He had not known this was to be a ceremony for the giving of extravagant gifts; and even if he had, what could the adopted son of a poor fisherman offer to compare with these treasures?

After all the other guests had risen to make their presentations, the king turned to Perseus. "Well, Perseus," he said. "Have we saved the best gift for last? Tell us, what have *you* brought me . . . boy?"

Perseus rose from his chair. He did not know what to say. He realized now that the king had set out to deliberately humiliate him, and his face burned red with embarrassment.

"Perhaps, Sire, my gift *is* the greatest of all, for it cannot be bought at any price. You know I have no riches to share with you, no storehouses of treasure, or stables of horses from which to choose my gift. But I will give you a gift that costs me more dearly than any of these — the gift of my own strength and courage. Anything you wish me to do, I will do for you!"

The crowd was silent. Polydectes studied the youth standing before him for a long moment. Finally he set down his goblet and spoke calmly. "All right," he said. "I want you to bring me the head of Medusa."

The other guests gasped, then some began to laugh. Surely the king was making a joke — no mortal dared even approach Medusa, or *any* of the deadly Gorgon sisters! Medusa's hair was made of writhing snakes, and the very act of looking upon her face turned mortal men to stone.

But Polydectes did not laugh, nor did Perseus. They were playing a deadly game, a game of pride. And Polydectes was winning.

Perseus looked around at the other guests. The laughter had stopped, and all eyes were fixed on the brash young man. He turned back to the king and saw the same evil half-smile he had first seen when Polydectes had spoken of his mother.

"Well?" said the king.

"I will do it," Perseus said. "I will bring you the head of Medusa."

And the crowd watched in stunned silence as Perseus turned and marched out of the hall.

"I am an idiot!" Perseus said to the sea. The full moon danced on the waves as the young man sat on the sand, agonizing over his boastful promise to Polydectes. "I am a proud, arrogant fool! How could I promise to slay Medusa? I am not a warrior, I am a fisherman! What shall I do? Shall I wander over the world, blindly casting my net about, hoping to snare a Gorgon? I don't even know where the Gorgons live! I am an idiot!"

Perseus scooped up a handful of sand and hurled it into the waves. The moonlight shining on the water created a luminous path that seemed to lead all the way beyond the horizon, out to the open sea.

"Well, one thing is certain: I cannot go home. What would I do, tell the funny story at breakfast of how I have brought shame on myself and my whole family by making a promise I won't be able to keep? Or should I simply announce that I won't be going out to fish today, because I have to go cut off the head of Medusa? Ohhh! I am an idiot!"

And so, that very night, Perseus set out to seek advice from the only one he could think of who was wise enough to aid him in his quest.

4

The Search for Medusa

"**W**ise priestess, I have traveled all night with a fearful, troubled heart. I have made a foolish promise, but I feel I must try to carry it through." As he spoke to the Oracle, Perseus did not know he stood in the very spot where his grandfather had heard the terrible prophecy so many years before.

Perseus bowed his head. "I seek to slay the Gorgon Medusa," he said, "and I ask your guidance."

"I am not your guide," intoned the Oracle in her hollow voice. "But guides you shall have. Follow the wisdom of two from Mt. Olympus."

"Gods?" said Perseus, looking up. "I will be helped by the gods?" The Oracle nodded, and Perseus' spirits began to rise. "Which gods will help me?" he asked.

"One winged, one with gray eyes," said the Oracle, and the mist began to thicken and swirl around her.

"Wait!" said Perseus. "Where do I find them? How. . . ?"

But the Oracle did not answer. The mist had engulfed her completely, and when a sudden gust of wind blew the mist away, she was gone.

Perseus stared at the empty altar for a moment, then turned and headed wearily back down the mountain. The surge of hope he had felt when the Oracle promised him the help of the gods was fading rapidly. He had hoped the Oracle would tell him exactly how to proceed, and prophesy the success or failure of his quest; instead her message had been vague and cryptic, and he knew almost as little now as when he had set out to seek her counsel.

"One does not visit the gods unbidden," Perseus muttered as he stumbled over the mountain rocks. "And besides, where would I find them? I don't even know where to find the Gorgons!"

Perseus kicked the ground, cursing for the hundredth time his rash promise to Polydectes. He longed to be close to home again, fishing with Dictys, and his heart ached as he pictured Danae's grief when she learned of his secret departure in the night.

Perseus' thoughts were interrupted when he felt something thump him sharply on the head.

"What? Who's that?" he cried, turning to look behind him. But no one was there. Suddenly there was the sound of running footsteps on the path in front of him. Perseus whirled about; again, no one was there.

But as Perseus stared down the path,

a glittering object began to take form in the distance. The sound of rich music filled the air, and the object grew brighter and brighter, until Perseus had to shield his eyes. The radiant form then began to move so rapidly up the path that Perseus was afraid it would engulf him completely in flames. He fell to his knees and covered his head.

"Young Perseus, stand and prepare to meet your guide." The voice was deep and commanding. It seemed to come from the center of the fireball. Still shielding his eyes, Perseus rose timidly to his feet.

Then suddenly the light was gone, and the woods rang with impish laughter. Perseus looked up, and standing before him was a grinning young man with wings on his ankles and a golden wand in his hand.

"Greetings, Perseus," the man said, his eyes twinkling. "Hermes, here to do your bidding."

Hermes bowed deeply and, clicking his heels, rose a few feet into the air.

Of course, thought Perseus, this was the winged god the Oracle had prophesied. Hermes, son of Zeus and Maia, the trickster god, the master thief of Olympus.

"Do you know of my quest?" said Perseus.

"Certainly," said Hermes, fluttering back down to earth. "That is why I am here. I have a gift for you, my friend."

Hermes reached beneath his cloak and pulled out a huge curved sword. As Perseus watched, Hermes flew to where a giant oak towered above the mountain path. Gripping the sword's handle with both hands, the fleet-footed god swung the steely blade through the air. The sword sliced cleanly through the huge trunk, and the great oak fell to the ground with a thunderous crash.

Laughing, Hermes glided back to where Perseus stood gaping at the fallen tree. "This is the right tool for your job," Hermes said, handing Perseus the sword. "It cannot be bent or broken by the monster's scales. Use it well, and Medusa's head will be yours."

Perseus took the sword and swung it through the air in front of him. The weapon was heavy, but perfectly balanced; the handle felt good in Perseus' hands.

"But how can I ever get close enough to use it if the Gorgon's face turns all living things to stone?"

"A good question, an excellent question," said Hermes, nodding and scratching his head. He looked off into the distance, then up at the sky. "Sister," he called loudly toward the heavens. "Sister, we need you now!"

Suddenly the wind picked up, and the birds cried out warnings in the gusty air. The sky turned metal gray, as if in anticipation of a great storm. There was a clap of thunder, and in a blinding flash

of light, a muscular young woman holding a gleaming bronze shield appeared before Perseus.

"Pallas Athena, my sister," whispered Hermes. "She is very strong — it was she who first tamed horses for men to ride."

"So, this is the boy," Athena said, her gray eyes flashing. "The one who bragged he could kill Medusa. What an astonishing claim, Perseus."

Perseus felt his face grow red. "I know," he said. "I fear it is impossible. For how can I slay her if I can't even look at her to see where to swing my sword? It was not a very smart promise to make."

A slight smile crossed the goddess' face. She glanced at Hermes, then thrust her shining bronze shield toward Perseus. "Look at your face, Perseus," she commanded.

The polished bronze of the shield was so shiny that Perseus could easily see his reflection. He looked tired and frightened. Embarrassed, he turned away.

"Look again!" Athena commanded.

Perseus stole another glance at his frightened reflection, and again he turned away.

"Forget your fear, Perseus," said the goddess, her voice softer. "Don't you understand? This is how you shall see the monster. You must never look upon her directly — but look into the shield and see *her* reflection as you can see your own now. That is how you will know where to swing your sword."

Athena thrust the shield toward Perseus. "Take it," she said.

Perseus took the shield from Athena. "Thank you," he said.

"Now I must go," said Athena. "Good luck and good-bye to both of you." And with that, the great goddess rose from the ground and vanished in a flash of Zeus' lightning.

Perseus stared at the empty sky for

a moment; then, taking a deep breath, he turned to Hermes. "Well, let us go," he said.

"Where?" said Hermes.

"To the monster."

"But you are far from ready, Perseus! You have a sword, and a shield with which to look upon the monster. But how will you keep the monster and her awful sisters from seeing *you*? And once you have Medusa's head, how will you carry it? For even when the head is cut from her body, to look directly at her face would mean death! And you must venture far over impassable mountains and uncharted oceans to reach the Gorgons. How will you travel there and back? Have you thought of that?"

Speechless, Perseus shook his head.

"Well, let's think," said Hermes. "You will need a means to make yourself invisible. You will need a magic bag in which to carry Medusa's head and protect yourself from its deadly gaze. And, as for travel, it would be nice, wouldn't it, if you could fly? So you need a pair of winged sandals to give you that power."

Perseus looked helplessly at Hermes. "Where could I possibly. . . ?"

"Ah," said Hermes. "Fortunately all these gifts are in the possession of the Nymphs of the North. And I am sure they would gladly give them to you. They are a very generous people."

"Really?" said Perseus.

Hermes nodded. "Yes. But unfortunately, I do not know where the Nymphs of the North live."

"Oh," said Perseus. "Then I guess I'm back where I started."

"Do not despair, Perseus," said Hermes. "You give up too easily. Take my hand. We will fly to the Land of Twilight, to the ones who can point the way. But let me warn you to be prepared — "

"For what?" asked Perseus.

"For the sight you are about to see there," said Hermes, his eyes flashing. "It may give you nightmares for the rest of your life."

5

The Gray Women

There was no dawn in the Land of Twilight. The sky was dark gray as Hermes and Perseus hovered in the misty air, Perseus clinging tightly to Hermes' cloak. The two had flown all night without stopping, but Perseus was not tired. Winging through the air beside the messenger god, over oceans and rocky cliffs, over forests and villages and fields had been the most exhilarating experience of his life.

Now, breathless, Perseus peered toward the cliffside where the trickster pointed with his wand. "They're out," said Hermes. "Look."

Perseus looked far up the cliff to the

rocky ledge where Hermes pointed, the highest ledge above the sea. Perched there at the mouth of a cave were three grotesque creatures, screeching and cackling in the misty fog. The creatures were half-bird and half-human; swan-shaped, but with human heads, and beneath their wings, arms and hands.

"The Gray Women," said Hermes, "the ones who will help you next. Listen to them. . . ."

Two of the bird-women had begun cackling especially loudly, bickering over something the third grasped tightly in her gnarled hand. "Give it to me," screeched the first, her bony arm outstretched. "It is my turn to have it!"

"No!" screeched the other, fluttering her wings. "I need it! Let me have it next! Me!"

Hermes turned to Perseus with a devilish grin. "Can you guess what they are fighting about?" he asked.

"No," breathed Perseus.

"Look closely." Hermes pointed back to the ledge. The third bird-woman opened her clawlike hand to reveal a large, round, dripping, white object. "Take it," she cackled and, with a screech of triumph, one of the other creatures snatched the dripping object and clapped it to her forehead.

"It is an eyeball," Hermes whispered, "the only one they have."

"What?" stammered Perseus. "An eye?"

"It's true," whispered Hermes. "All day they pass it back and forth. One eye among the three of them to look upon this gloomy land. . . ."

Perseus turned back to the ledge. The creature who had taken the eye was peering down the mountainside, cackling out descriptions of the valley below. Perseus shook his head in wonderment, then turned back to Hermes. "Well, tell me what I must do," he whispered.

Moments later, Perseus stood alone at the top of the granite cliff, overlooking the ledge where the bird-women were nestled before their cave. Shivering in the foggy mist, he watched them pass the giant, dripping eyeball from one to the other, each sister taking her turn inserting the eye into a gaping hole in her wrinkled forehead.

Perseus held his breath. He waited until one of the women removed the eyeball from her socket, and before she could pass it to her sister — in a moment when *all* of them were blind — he leaped down and snatched the wet and oozing eyeball from the gnarled, outstretched hand.

The eye felt cold and slimy in Perseus' hand. Gingerly Perseus held it away from his body and listened as the creatures began to screech among themselves, each believing one of the others had stolen their most precious possession. When finally they realized that none of them possessed the eye, their cackling turned to ear-piercing cries.

"Silence!" Perseus commanded. "*I* have your eye!"

The bird-women fell silent. No one but themselves had ever been on their ledge before. Blindly they craned their necks toward the sound of Perseus' voice.

"Give it back," one of the creatures whimpered. "Whoever you are, you must give it back!"

"I will give it back, but on one condition. You must tell me where to find the Hyperboreans, the Nymphs of the North."

The bird-women fell silent again. This was sacred knowledge. The Hyperboreans were an eternally joyful people, living in everlasting happiness far apart from the rest of the mortal world. It was a crime against the gods to reveal the whereabouts of their blissful land.

"We don't know where they live," whined one of the sisters. "No one does. Now give us back our eye, our eye!"

"You lie!" shouted Perseus. "You know where they live, and how to get there! And you will tell me, or you shall never look upon these gray skies again! I will hurl this ugly eye into the sea!"

"No!" shrieked the sisters. "Give it back, and we will tell you! But it will do you no good, for you cannot travel there by ship or by land. . . ."

"Never mind how I will travel, but tell me quickly where I must go — or else prepare to spend the rest of your wretched lives in hollow darkness!"

And so the three gray sisters told Perseus how to go beyond the lofty mountains to the back of the North Wind, to the peaceful country of Hyperborea. When they finished their directions, Perseus stepped forward and held out the watery eyeball.

"Take back your vision, lady birds. . . ."

Perseus gently placed the eye into the outstretched hand of one of the sisters and, even as he climbed back up the cliff to meet Hermes, he could hear their cackling voices squabbling over who should have it next.

"They told me everything we need to know!" Perseus shouted as he joined the messenger god in the valley below the cliffs.

"Congratulations!" shouted Hermes.

"Can you take me to the back of the North Wind?"

"With pleasure!" Hermes laughed and, grabbing Perseus' arm, he swept him high into the sky. And with more confidence than he had felt in days, Perseus traveled with the quicksilver god away from the gloomy Land of Twilight toward the blessed country of the Hyperboreans.

6

The Nymphs of the North

The fields of Hyperborea were filled with wildflowers. Their brilliant colors seemed to explode in the late afternoon sun as Perseus and Hermes touched softly down in the high grass. Perseus could hear the music of flutes and lyres in the distance, and a gentle breeze filled the air with sweet flower perfume. Perseus closed his eyes, and a feeling of great peace washed over him. In that moment, he felt he would be content to stay there forever.

Hermes touched Perseus' arm. "Do not forget why we have come, my friend," he said gently. "Follow me."

Perseus followed Hermes along a winding path through the fields toward the ringing music. On a hill in the distance he could see a bonfire blazing, and around the fire were several dancing figures. "There must be a celebration here tonight," he said as they approached the camp.

"I am told there is a celebration here *every* night," Hermes said. "And there is always plenty of food and drink, and no one is ever sick, and no one ever grows old."

"Then it is no wonder they choose to remain hidden from the rest of the world," said Perseus. "I hope they will receive us kindly."

"Do not worry, my friend," said Hermes, smiling. "The Nymphs of the North have never learned how to be unkind."

Hermes waved his wand in the air and called out toward the nymphs celebrating by the bonfire. "Helloooo. . . ."

The music stopped, and the nymphs looked across the field toward Perseus and Hermes. Then, in a joyful flurry, they all rushed down the path to greet them. Before he knew what was happening, Perseus found himself surrounded by dozens of beautiful young women laughing, singing, and tugging him playfully toward their camp. As they led him toward the fire, some of the nymphs wove flowers into his hair; others whispered their sweet, joyful songs into his ears.

The nymphs prepared a great feast for their two visitors, chattering and laughing all the while. Perseus and Hermes dined on roasted meats, dates, and figs with honey. And as Perseus listened to the music and the delightful chatter of the Hyperboreans, Medusa and the task that lay before him seemed very far away.

But finally the feast was over and Hermes called aross the fire to Perseus.

"Tell them why we have come, my friend," he said, "or I fear we shall never be able to leave. . . ."

Perseus knew that what Hermes said was true; reluctantly he stood up and addressed the nymphs.

"Beautiful ladies, I feel I would be happy to stay with you here forever — "

"Oh, do!" cried the nymphs, interrupting. "Do stay! You are very welcome here!"

Perseus looked helplessly at Hermes. Grinning, Hermes shrugged and nodded to Perseus to continue.

"Alas, we cannot stay," said Perseus, "for I have made a promise to my king. I must slay the Gorgon Medusa, and I have come to ask for your help."

"Oh, yes," cried the nymphs. "We will help you, of course we will help you. But first, tell us your story, then we will do everything we can."

And so Perseus told the nymphs the story of his boastful promise to Polydectes; of how he had journeyed to the Oracle of Delphi, how he had been met by Hermes and Athena, and how he had learned the way to the Hyperborean paradise by stealing the eye of the three Gray Sisters. The nymphs listened attentively and clapped when he had finished his tale, then huddled together to discuss what they could do to help him in his quest.

"We think we can provide you with everything you need," one of the nymphs said to Perseus as several others scurried off into the woods. "But you must promise to be very careful, and to visit us again someday when you have completed your task."

Perseus looked into the nymph's pretty face and smiled. "That is a promise I will joyfully keep," he said.

"Good," said the nymph, her eyes shining. "Then let me show you what we have found for you."

The other nymphs had returned from

the forest with a large chest, which they set in front of the fire. The first nymph reached inside and pulled out an oddly shaped satchel. "This bag is magical," she said, handing the satchel to Perseus. "It will change its size and shape to carry whatever you put inside."

"The head of Medusa," breathed Perseus.

"Yes," said the nymph.

Perseus strapped the bag over his shoulder. "Thank you," he said, but when he looked up, there was no one there. Perseus looked around, confused. Where had the nymph gone?

"This is the cap of darkness. You can see that it works very well." Perseus heard the nymph's voice clearly, but she was nowhere to be seen.

"It, too, is magical, Perseus. When you wear it, as I am now, you will be quite invisible, and can approach and escape from the Gorgons unseen. Watch. I shall remove it now."

Perseus stared in astonishment as the nymph materialized before his eyes, holding a green plumed cap. She handed him the cap, then turned back to the chest.

"And, finally, we have found these for you. . . ."

The nymph reached into the chest and pulled out a pair of soft leather sandals. At each ankle fluttered a pair of tiny wings. "Wear these, and you shall be able to fly through the heavens as swiftly and surely as your winged companion."

The nymph handed Perseus the sandals and he eagerly slipped them on. In an instant the sandals flew up into the air, jerking Perseus aloft with them. For a moment the young man hung suspended upside down above the fire.

Hermes howled with laughter. "Practice, my boy, practice!" he shouted.

The nymphs giggled as Perseus struggled to bring his new powers of flight under control. With a great kick he managed to turn himself upright in the air; then, moving very gently, he began to circle the fire.

Hermes applauded as Perseus soared higher and higher above his head. Though clumsy at first, it wasn't long before Perseus was joyfully swooping through the trees, flying upside down and turning somersaults. Then, as he glided effortlessly through the purple twilight sky, waving at Hermes and the Hyperboreans below, the smile left his face. He realized there was no longer any reason to delay his journey to the Gorgons — and the task that lay before him now was terrifying.

7

The Gorgons

The terrible sisters were asleep. The three giant winged bodies lay sprawled on the deserted shore of their remote island — shiny scales glistening in the morning sun, claws shining with the luster of polished brass.

Perseus stared at the Gorgons' reflection in Athena's shield. Of the three, Medusa was by far the most awful: the vipers about her hideous face writhed incessantly in the hot island air, and the fangs that hung from her twisted, grinning mouth were the color of ocher.

"Look," whispered Hermes, nodding toward the stretch of beach be-

yond the Gorgons. "Do you see the statues?"

Perseus looked down the beach. The barren shore was dotted with stony figures, all frozen in odd, contorted poses. Most seemed to be running — some were covering their faces; others were looking back over their shoulders as they ran.

"Victims of Medusa," whispered Hermes. "Turned to stone when they looked upon her face."

Perseus stared at the statue figures in horror. The legends were true; Medusa's forces were deadly, and Perseus wondered if even the guidance of the gods could save him from her awesome power.

Hermes put his hand on Perseus' shoulder. "Well," he said. "Are you ready?"

Perseus did not speak, but continued to stare down the beach.

"You have a steely sword, a goddess' shield, winged sandals, a magic bag, and a cap to make you invisible," Hermes said. "You have everything you need, my boy."

"Yes," said Perseus. "Everything but courage." Perseus turned to Hermes, ashamed to finally admit his fear to the god who had become his friend.

Hermes gave Perseus a long, serious look. "Perseus," he said, "the secret is this: You will gain your courage as you attempt to succeed in your quest. One never has all his courage when he starts out. But he chooses a quest that will bring forth the courage that hides now behind veils of fear."

Perseus looked back at the Gorgons' reflection in his shield. "But how can I approach Medusa without waking the others?" he said, his voice shaking.

Hermes smiled. "Slowly and carefully," he said, "one step at a time. Keep your eyes on the shield and move like a silent warrior."

Perseus nodded but did not move.

"You can do it, Perseus," Hermes said. "You *can* defeat this monster. For, like me, you are a son of Zeus."

Perseus looked up. "What?"

"It is true. Many years ago, Zeus, your father and mine, came to your mother's bronze chamber in a shower of gold. He watches you now, and will be proud."

Hermes held Perseus' astonished gaze for a moment, then nodded toward the Gorgons. "Good luck, brother," he said.

The snakes of Medusa hissed and spat poison as Perseus made his way across the scorching sand. Staring into Athena's shield, the young man approached the hideous monster sideways, terrified that each step might wake her from her slumber. Step by careful step, he drew nearer and nearer, silently placing one sandaled foot and then the other down on the hot sand.

At last he was close enough to strike.

He could smell the monster's foul breath as he raised his sword high above his head, his arm trembling under the weight. Then, staring unblinking at Medusa's reflection in the shield, Perseus swept the mighty sword through the hot air, and in a single stroke he severed the monster's head from her body.

A horrible sound escaped from Medusa's fanged, leering mouth, and her blood gushed onto the sand. Her two monster sisters stirred at the noise and, waking to find their sister's headless, bloody body sprawled on the sand beside them, they reared up in horror.

Perseus grabbed frantically for the writhing snakes of Medusa's hair. He stuffed her severed head into his magic satchel as the two other Gorgons began to thrash about angrily in search of their sister's murderer. But Perseus pulled the cap of darkness from beneath his cloak; and before the monsters could descend on him, he vanished from their sight.

Only the satchel containing Medusa's head could be seen dangling in the air as Perseus flew high above the island. He watched the Gorgons thrashing about below him, until he could no longer see them through the heavy clouds floating high in the morning sky. Then, pausing in the air, he pulled off the cap of darkness and held Medusa's head up to the heavens, as if it were a trophy he wanted his father Zeus to see. Then he remembered Hermes.

Perseus looked around him in the clouds, but the messenger god was nowhere to be seen. And somehow Perseus knew that his quicksilver guide had left him and would not return. Now a hero in his own right, Perseus was on his own.

8

The Princess

Perseus flew triumphantly toward home. He flew over half the world: past cloud-covered mountains, past the constellations of the Bear and the Crab, past the chariot of Helios the sun god. But as he flew over the ocean near Ethiopia, buffeted by gentle breezes, he looked down and saw a horrifying sight: a beautiful girl chained to a rocky ledge near the shore.

Perseus flew down and hovered above the girl. Her hair was blowing in the wind and though tears ran down her cheeks, she stood as motionless as an ebony statue.

"Beautiful maiden," called Perseus. "Who are you?"

"I am Andromeda, daughter of Queen Cassiopeia! But do not call me beautiful! You may anger the gods! And you see before you what the anger of the gods can bring."

"But you *are* beautiful! I shout it to the heavens! Why are you bound here?"

"It is my mother's fault," cried Andromeda above the waves. "She boasted that she and I were both more beautiful than Poseidon's daughters. This enraged Poseidon, and indeed, all the gods — for how could a mortal girl be as beautiful as the nymphs of the sea?"

"I have never seen a sea nymph," shouted Perseus, "but I suspect your mother was right, for these mortal eyes have never looked on such beauty as yours."

"Oh, do not say so," wept Andromeda, turning her face away. "In his rage, Poseidon sent a great plague on our country of Ethiopia, and now only my sacrifice to the sea monster will lift his curse from our land. Bid me farewell and be on your way, for I fear there is no help for me."

Perseus felt his heart break and at the same time he felt it soar — for he was falling in love with the princess, and his love filled him with a strength he'd never known before. "I will not leave you — now or ever!" he shouted. "Let the sea monster come for you! Let this son of Zeus see the beast that dare harm you!"

Before Andromeda could speak, a horrible sound erupted from the waves and the head of the hideous sea dragon broke through the water.

Andromeda began to shriek madly as Perseus swooped down and hacked at the monster's barnacled back with Hermes' sword. The serpent plunged toward him, poison dripping from its deadly fangs, but Perseus darted out of the way.

Again Perseus dove toward the serpent, slashing at its back and spiny tail with his sword. Vomiting up blood and salt water, the serpent once more turned viciously to attack. As Perseus swooped out of the reach of the deadly fangs, he realized he could only wound the monster by hacking at its back and tail. The way to slay the beast was to cut off its head. But how could he get close enough?

Hovering in the air, Perseus watched the sun sparkling on the water, and suddenly he had an idea. He zoomed down toward the serpent, and as the creature reared back to lunge for him, Perseus pulled on the cap of darkness.

The sea serpent looked about, bewildered by the sudden disappearance of its attacker. Perseus soared invisibly toward the sun. Then he pulled off his cap and, twisting and spinning in the air, Perseus caused his shadow to dance across the waves below.

The monster let out a hideous roar and attacked the shadow, burying its face in the waves. Perseus swooped down, and with the same single stroke that had killed Medusa, he hacked off the monster's head.

The sea flowed red with the serpent's blood as Perseus loosened Andromeda's chains. Then he took the princess in his arms, and as he held her and kissed her wet face and stroked her wind-tossed hair, her weeping and trembling gradually ceased. And when Perseus asked the princess to marry him, she whispered, "Yes, I will."

The Ethiopian night was lit with torches, and garlands of flowers hung from the palace ceiling. Festive music filled the palace hall as the great doors swung open to admit the bride and bridegroom to their splendid wedding banquet.

As Perseus feasted with his bride and

her family, he told them about King Polydectes and about slaying the Gorgon; he told them about the Gray Women and the Nymphs of the North, and about his journeys over land and sea.

Sitting beside his beautiful bride, Perseus felt like a great hero. And as the candlelight dimmed and the music faded to the sound of a single flute, he thought of Hermes and wished his half brother could see him now.

Perseus rose early and stepped softly onto the balcony of the royal bedchamber to watch the sun come up over the distant hills. Sensing her husband gone, Andromeda woke. In her bare feet, she joined him in the light of dawn. "What troubles you, my love?" she asked, gently taking his arm.

Perseus turned to his new wife and looked into her dark eyes. "I must return to my mother's island," he said.

"My quest is only half-complete. There is a gift I must give my king."

"The gift of Medusa's head?"

Perseus nodded.

"May I go with you?"

"How can you, my sweet? I must fly."

"I will cling to you through the heavens, help you carry your sword and shield, your satchel — "

"But what about the danger? I cannot lead you into danger, Andromeda."

"The danger I face if I go with you will be less than my sorrow if I do not."

Perseus smiled at his wife. "Then let us leave before the others wake," he said. "Your parents will never forgive me for taking you away so soon — and through the air, no less."

The two of them laughed and held each other tightly in the early amber light.

9

The Deadly Power of Medusa

The gate to Dictys' yard banged in the wind, and a skinny cat cried by the front door. Inside the cottage, there was no sign of Danae or of the old fisherman and his wife. The house and hearth looked as if they'd been neglected for weeks: small animals had nested in the cupboards, and the stone floor was covered with a layer of dust and sand.

"The fisherman's wife swept every day," said Perseus, his heart pounding. "Where are they? Where?"

"Who shouts in there?" came a raspy voice from the courtyard.

Perseus and Andromeda stepped out

into the bright sunlight to find an old man standing in the yard. Perseus recognized him as a peddler who had traveled about the island for many years.

"Who goes there?" the feeble man asked, squinting at the young couple.

"Perseus, son of Danae," said Perseus.

"Ah, young Perseus!" The old man's face lit up. "Of course! Welcome! Now go — " he said, pushing Perseus with his gnarled hands. "Go and rescue your mother and the man who was like a father to you!"

"Where are they?" cried Perseus.

"They're hiding — hiding in Demeter's temple."

"Why?"

"After you left, my boy, there was terrible trouble. Polydectes asked your mother to marry him and she refused — and the wounded tyrant turned his fury against your household. He terrorized your family until the old woman died of fright, and your mother and Dictys fled to the temple where the priestesses of Demeter now hide them and care for them."

Perseus stared at the peddler for a moment, then he picked up his satchel. "Go with him to the temple, my love," he said to Andromeda. "Tell my mother I will be with her soon. But first I must deliver a gift."

As Perseus entered the palace, he could hear the voices of the men in the banquet hall: They were toasting Polydectes, laughing raucously, trying to please the brute with loud praise.

Perseus strode through the entrance of the big room, and the voices fell silent. He stood very still as all eyes turned to stare at him. Hermes' sword was buckled about his waist, and he held Athena's shield in one hand, the nymphs' satchel in the other.

Polydectes glared at the youth. "Get out of here!" he shouted drunkenly. "I don't care about you anymore!"

"Ah, but you never did care about me," Perseus said. "You only sent me for Medusa's head to get me out of your way. You thought my quest would certainly cause my death! And it would have, had the gods not favored me."

"What's he talking about?" Polydectes asked his lieutenants, slurring his words.

"I am saying that I have succeeded!" shouted Perseus.

"What? Succeeded at what?"

"Look. I have brought you the gift of your heart's desire."

Polydectes began to understand — but before he could turn away or even shield his eyes, Perseus yanked the severed head of Medusa from his satchel and held it high in the air for all to see.

And all did see; and as they did, each

man turned to a statue of stone. Polydectes, the cruel ruler, was frozen for all time with a look of stark terror on his face — the coward finally exposed and the son of Zeus revenged.

10

The End
of the Journey

"Now tell us, my son," Danae said, "when did Athena and Hermes leave your side?"

Perseus, Andromeda, Danae, and Dictys sat bathed in the light of the cottage hearth fire, their faces glowing with the joy of being together.

"As soon as Athena gave me her shield, she vanished," Perseus said, "and I no longer saw Hermes after I started toward Medusa. But even though I could not see them, they both seemed to be with me when I killed the Gorgon, and when I killed the sea serpent, and when I turned Polydectes to stone. In fact, I feel they are with us in spirit right now."

Dictys smiled. "Indeed, Perseus," he said. "Now that we are all together, I think I do feel the presence of the gods in our little cottage."

"Do you?" asked Perseus with a twinkle in his eye. "Then can you also sense what one just whispered in my ear about who should be the next king of our island?"

"Ah, the voice said *you* no doubt," said Dictys.

Perseus shook his head and pointed at Dictys. "No, the voice said that *Dictys* — the one who saved Perseus and Danae from death many years ago — *he* should be king."

Dictys laughed and shook his head. "No, no, if that is what you heard, then it is only Hermes up to one of his tricks."

"No, not Hermes," Perseus said softly. "It was the gray-eyed goddess who spoke to me just now, the protector of cities and favorite daughter of Zeus."

"And what exactly did Athena say, my son?" asked Danae.

"She says it is Zeus' will that Dictys rule — for Dictys did Zeus' job of raising me when the great god could not do it himself — and Dictys did the job very well."

"But I do not know how to rule!" sputtered Dictys. "I'm just a humble fisherman!"

"Only a truly humble man can shine with the light of real wisdom," said Andromeda.

"Well said, my dear," said Danae, smiling at her new daughter-in-law. "Dictys, I do not think you can ignore the request of a goddess."

"Then it is decided!" Perseus said, rising. "I will go tell the people of the island that Dictys will be our new king!"

Andromeda followed Perseus to the door. As she bid her husband good-bye, she whispered in his ear, "Athena really spoke to you?"

Perseus smiled. "The goddess has a very soft whisper, my love. Whether it was a breeze brushing by — or truly her voice, I do not know."

Soon after making Dictys king of the island, Perseus spoke with his mother about returning to Greece to see her father, Acrisius. "These many years may have softened his feelings toward us," Perseus said.

Danae looked away, and Perseus touched her arm.

"Don't you want to see him again, just to be reconciled with him?" he asked.

"The things he did to us were unforgivable," Danae said.

"Yes. But fear can move us all to terrible extremes. And we turned out all right, didn't we? What need do we have now to bear a grudge against him? Mother, you should see your father before he dies. Otherwise, you will carry the burden of your anger toward him all your life."

Danae nodded. "All right, my son. With you and Andromeda at my side, perhaps I can face whatever must be faced."

And so Perseus, Andromeda, and Danae set out together for the kingdom of Greece. But when they arrived, they discovered that King Acrisius had been driven from the city by his enemies. No one seemed to know where the king had fled; so, disappointed, the three decided there was nothing to do but return home.

As they prepared to set sail for their island, Perseus was told of a great athletic contest being held in the north, in a land called Larissa. "It is not far out of our way," Perseus told Andromeda and Danae. "I would like to drop anchor there and enter the games."

The two women agreed this would be an exciting venture, for Perseus was

an excellent athlete, and winning such a contest would bring great honor to their island. They set sail at once, docking the next day near the kingdom of Larissa.

The sporting arena at Larissa was filled with cheering spectators. Andromeda and Danae sat high in the stands and watched as Perseus stepped forward to take his turn in the discus-throwing competition. Grasping the oval-shaped discus, Perseus drew back his arm and hurled the discus through the sunlit sky. But as the crowd watched and cheered, the discus swerved unpredictably from its path and landed in the crowded stands.

The spectators cried out in horror, and Perseus, Danae, and Andromeda rushed to the spot where the discus had landed. There they found a crowd gathered around an old man lying on the ground, unconscious from the blow of Perseus' discus.

The king of Larissa was bending over the dying man, lamenting the terrible accident that had befallen his guest at the contest. As Perseus pushed forward to offer his horrified apologies, he heard the king of Larissa say, "All stand back from Acrisius!"

"Acrisius?" cried Perseus, grasping the arm of the king. "Is that Acrisius, King of Greece?"

"He was once the king of Greece, until he was deposed," said the king of Larissa. "These games were to be in honor of his visit — now they will be in honor of his death."

Danae and Perseus knelt beside the old man. "Father!" Danae cried. "It is your daughter, Danae! And it was your grandson who did slay you, Father! It was an accident, Father — " she sobbed. "But the prophecy of the Oracle could not be changed!"

The king's dying eyes seemed to flash with recognition and love as he looked upon Danae's grieving face; and when the old man's eyes rested on Perseus, a sad and bitter smile flickered across his lips. Then he did not breathe again.

Perseus, Andromeda, and Danae returned home, and soon afterward Perseus and Andromeda had a child they named Electryon — who would someday be the grandfather of the great Greek hero, Hercules.

Perseus gave the Gorgon's head to his favorite goddess, Athena, and Athena welded it to her mighty shield to help her in battle. Perseus, the hero, his troubles and quest having come to an end, had no more need for the deadly power of Medusa.

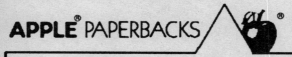

APPLE® PAPERBACKS

Pick an Apple and Polish Off Some Great Reading!

BEST-SELLING APPLE TITLES

❏ MT43944-8	**Afternoon of the Elves** Janet Taylor Lisle	**$2.75**
❏ MT43109-9	**Boys Are Yucko** Anna Grossnickle Hines	**$2.75**
❏ MT43473-X	**The Broccoli Tapes** Jan Slepian	**$2.95**
❏ MT42709-1	**Christina's Ghost** Betty Ren Wright	**$2.75**
❏ MT43461-6	**The Dollhouse Murders** Betty Ren Wright	**$2.75**
❏ MT43444-6	**Ghosts Beneath Our Feet** Betty Ren Wright	**$2.75**
❏ MT44351-8	**Help! I'm a Prisoner in the Library** Eth Clifford	**$2.75**
❏ MT44567-7	**Leah's Song** Eth Clifford	**$2.75**
❏ MT43618-X	**Me and Katie (The Pest)** Ann M. Martin	**$2.75**
❏ MT41529-8	**My Sister, The Creep** Candice F. Ransom	**$2.75**
❏ MT42883-7	**Sixth Grade Can Really Kill You** Barthe DeClements	**$2.75**
❏ MT40409-1	**Sixth Grade Secrets** Louis Sachar	**$2.75**
❏ MT42882-9	**Sixth Grade Sleepover** Eve Bunting	**$2.75**
❏ MT41732-0	**Too Many Murphys** Colleen O'Shaughnessy McKenna	**$2.75**

Available wherever you buy books, or use this order form.

- -

Scholastic Inc., P.O. Box 7502, 2931 East McCarty Street, Jefferson City, MO 65102

Please send me the books I have checked above. I am enclosing $_____ (please add $2.00 to cover shipping and handling). Send check or money order — no cash or C.O.D.s please.

Name _____

Address _____

City_____ **State/Zip** _____

Please allow four to six weeks for delivery. Offer good in the U.S.A. only. Sorry, mail orders are not available to residents of Canada. Prices subject to change.

APP591